MAKING FRIENDS WITH MY EMOTIONS

IT'S OK TO BE CONFUSED

THERESA EMMINIZER

PowerKiDS press

Published in 2025 by The Rosen Publishing Group, Inc.
2544 Clinton Street, Buffalo, NY 14224

First Edition

Editor: Theresa Emminizer
Book Design: Michael Flynn

Photo Credits: Cover, p. 1 Dean Drobot/Shutterstock.com; (series background) Sergei Mishchenko/Shutterstock.com; p. 5 MZStock/Shutterstock.com; p. 7 BongkarnGraphic/Shutterstock.com; p. 9 Halfpoint/Shutterstock.com; pp. 11, 15 NadyaEugene/Shutterstock.com; p. 13 Red Stock/Shutterstock.com; p. 17 Alena Ozerova/Shutterstock.com; p. 19 fizkes/Shutterstock.com; p. 21 Olena Yakobchuk/Shutterstock.com.

Library of Congress Cataloging-in-Publication Data

Names: Emminizer, Theresa, author.
Title: It's ok to be confused / Theresa Emminizer.
Description: [Buffalo] : PowerKids Press, [2025] | Series: Making friends with my emotions | Includes bibliographical references and index. |
Audience: Grades K-1
Identifiers: LCCN 2023054214 (print) | LCCN 2023054215 (ebook) | ISBN 9781499444995 (library binding) | ISBN 9781499444988 (paperback) | ISBN 9781499445008 (ebook)
Subjects: LCSH: Uncertainty–Juvenile literature. | Comprehension in children–Juvenile literature. | Emotions in children–Juvenile literature.
Classification: LCC BF463.U5 E46 2025 (print) | LCC BF463.U5 (ebook) |
DDC 155.4/124–dc23/eng/20231218
LC record available at https://lccn.loc.gov/2023054214
LC ebook record available at https://lccn.loc.gov/2023054215

Manufactured in the United States of America

CONTENTS

Feeling Confused 4
Why We Feel Confused. 6
Confused and Alone 8
Don't Hide Away 10
Tell Somebody 12
Mixed Feelings 14
Coping with Confusion 16
You're Not Alone 18
Making Friends with Confusion 20
Glossary 22
For More Information 23
Index 24

Feeling Confused

What does it feel like to be confused? Your face might feel hot. Your stomach might turn. Your head might hurt. You might feel angry or **embarrassed** that you don't understand what's going on. Feeling confused can be uncomfortable. But don't worry! It's OK to be confused.

Why We Feel Confused

Confusion is a natural part of life. You don't have to be embarrassed of feeling confused or pretend to feel differently. In fact, hiding your confusion can be **harmful**. Confusion has an important job. It tells us that we need a little help!

Confused and Alone

Nova was confused. She was embarrassed to tell anyone, but she didn't understand what was going on in school. Nova felt all alone. Her classmates all seemed to know what to do. She started having bad stomachaches. She asked her mom if she could stay at home.

Don’t Hide Away!

When we **ignore** our feelings or push them down, it can make us feel sick. You don’t have to hide your feelings. You don’t have to let them control you either. Instead, try just noticing feelings: “I feel confused. That’s OK!”

Tell Somebody

When you're confused, it helps to talk to someone about how you're feeling. Share your thoughts and feelings with a grown-up you trust. A safe adult will never make you feel bad about being confused. They won't be mad at you. Safe adults listen and help!

Mixed Feelings

Roy's parents were **divorced**. Roy spent the weekends at his dad's place. Roy loved his dad very much. But he missed his mom's house. He missed his bedroom and his things. Roy felt confused. If he loved his dad, why didn't he want to stay with him?

Coping with Confusion

Sometimes we feel more than one way about a person or **situation**. That's called having mixed feelings, and it can be confusing! But feelings aren't right or wrong. They just are! Try drawing a picture of how you feel or writing about it in a journal.

You're Not Alone

Confusion can make you feel lonely. Like everyone else has it all figured out and you're the only one who doesn't. But remember, you're not alone. Everyone you know has felt confused at one time or another. Even grown-ups feel confused!

Making Friends with Confusion

Next time you feel confused, don't worry! Confusion is an important and healthy feeling. It's your body's way of telling you that it's time to ask for help. There's nothing to be embarrassed about. Remember, everybody feels confused sometimes! Share your feelings with the people you trust.

GLOSSARY

divorced: No longer married.

embarrassed: Feeling uncomfortable or ashamed.

harmful: Causing harm, or hurt.

ignore: To pretend something isn't happening.

situation: A set of events or the way things are.

FOR MORE INFORMATION

BOOKS

Bromage, Fran. *I Can Feel!* New York, NY: Rosen Publishing, 2023.

McAneney, Caitie. *I Use Mindfulness to Cope.* New York, NY: PowerKids Press, 2023.

WEBSITES

Kids Health
kidshealth.org/en/kids/talk-feelings.html
Learn how to name and talk about your feelings.

PBS Kids
pbskids.org/video/
Watch this helpful video about having mixed feelings.

Publisher's note to educators and parents: Our editors have carefully reviewed these websites to ensure that they are suitable for students. Many websites change frequently, however, and we cannot guarantee that a site's future contents will continue to meet our high standards of quality and educational value. Be advised that students should be closely supervised whenever they access the internet.

INDEX

H
help, 6, 12, 20
hide, 6, 10, 12

L
lonely, 18

N
natural, 6
notice, 10

U
uncomfortable, 4

W
worry, 20